FAILED LAWYER, POMPOUS ANGEL

By Donald W. Desaulniers

FAILED LAWYER, POMPOUS ANGEL

Table of Contents

CHAPTER 1 (Rotten Timing)

It was early evening on Friday, the 13th day of March, 2020 and I was angry. The Ontario premier had just announced that the whole bloody province was to be locked down for two weeks effective this coming Monday to stem the infection rate of the coronavirus pandemic which was ravaging most of the planet.

There were scads of rules and regulations dictating which businesses were to be deemed essential but at the moment I couldn't tell if I could remain open or not.

The timing was putrid. It had been a grossly quiet winter for business. I was an attorney whose main source of income was real estate transactions.

Normally business picked up quickly in April as the spring house market heated up.

Now this coronavirus crap was throwing a wrench into the gears of the entire economy.

As I finished washing and drying my supper dishes, it seemed prudent to grab a beer from the refrigerator and contemplate my future.

By the way, my name is Paul Lang and I'm still practising law at the ripe old age of seventy-two. I've been widowed for the past thirty years. Linda and I never had kids.

If she'd still been alive then I'm sure we would have retired together when I hit age sixty-five and began collecting my old age pension. Linda had been my legal secretary since shortly after we married in late 1979. Before that she had worked as a bank teller but hated the job.

When Linda got sick and passed away in February of 1990 just three months after her doctor discovered that her headaches were caused by a brain tumor, I continued running my small law office alone without any staff.

I've always been a bit of a failure as an attorney. I quickly learned that I wasn't swift enough on my feet to handle court trials. The other attorneys had no trouble mopping the floor with me so thereafter I restricted my law practice to office matters.

The bit of money I earned from the practice was quite pathetic and suddenly it appeared that 2020 would be a terrible year. Missing the spring real estate market would virtually guarantee that I'd have difficulty even generating enough fees to pay my office overhead.

By the time I'd polished off my third beer, I'd made my decision.

It was time to retire.

I tossed back a fourth beer before hitting the sack, rather pleased that I had made a major life decision. I'd almost retired last fall until procrastination and laziness persuaded me to continue slogging away for a while longer just to have something with which to fill my time.

On Saturday morning I got the termination process underway. I drove to my office and planned out what needed to be done.

My first call was to my landlord at his home. Curtis Black was also an attorney and I'd been renting my office from him for more than thirty years.

"Hi Curtis; it's Paul. After listening to the news last night about the imminent shutdown of society, I've decided to retire immediately. I'm sorry to bother you at home on Saturday but my tenancy runs from the 15th of each month. I've just emailed you a notice to vacate my office space effective April 14th and I've also slipped a hard copy under your office door."

Curtis was very gracious. He accepted my notice without any hassle and congratulated me on my decision to retire.

He also agreed to take over any ongoing files I couldn't finish off by the middle of April.

Embarrassingly I had to admit that my office had been so dreadfully slow since Christmas that there wouldn't likely be any active files left by April 14th.

We chatted for a while about how the shutdown might affect the local economy.

After we ended the call I got on the internet and downloaded from the Ontario Law Society's website the forms required to be completed in order for an attorney to close up his law practice.

CHAPTER 2 (Closing Up Shop)

For the remainder of Saturday and all day Sunday I worked on the office closure paperwork.

Disgustingly, there was only one active file in my entire office, a real estate sale scheduled to close on March 17th. I was already pretty much ready for closing unless the shutdown prevented lawyers from registering their real estate deals.

Because of that lack of business, it made more sense for me to close up my law practice effective March 23rd, 2020 which would give me a full week to wrap up any tag ends.

I also chose that date because it was the forty-seventh anniversary of my becoming a lawyer in Ontario back in 1973.

Despite the fact that my office rent would be paid to April 15th, I could save the annual dues and negligence insurance premiums for the period beginning on the date I closed the office.

I almost went to the Belleville casino for supper until I remembered that the facility was closing at midnight and remaining closed until the coronavirus lockdown was lifted in a couple of weeks. I didn't want to fight the crowds battling to find a slot machine.

In the end I watched Fox News on television until I got sick of all the hype about the virus. The whole world was in panic mode and it made me sick just listening to the dire predictions.

It seemed to me that no country could afford to shut down its economy for two weeks but that was what they were all doing. It sort of proved that politicians were nothing but lemmings rushing off the financial cliff in pathetic herds.

On Monday I learned from an e-mail sent by the Ontario Law Society that legal offices had been declared an essential service. That was a relief because it meant that my final real estate closing could take place tomorrow.

My landlord ran his own law practice from the same building. Curtis dropped in to see me on Monday afternoon.

"We didn't get a chance to talk on Saturday when you phoned, Paul. What do you think of these new restrictions on how we run our legal practices?"

"I'd hate them if I was sticking around but it just confirms to me that my timing in calling it quits is right. I've only got one sale to close tomorrow and that's the end of my active files. I've chosen next Monday the 23rd as my official retirement date because it's the anniversary of my original call to the bar in 1973."

"What do you plan to do with your office equipment and furniture?"

"I guess I'll take home anything I can use and give the rest to the Salvation Army."

"If it will make things easier
for you, I'd be happy to refund
your rent from March 23rd to April
14th and pay you $500 if you leave
everything except your computer
and personal effects."

"That would be great, Curtis. I
accept. Do you want to take over
my phone and fax numbers? My
practice is tiny but the clients I
have left are pretty loyal. I can
even leave my closed-out files.
I've been really proactive in
whittling them down. There's only
one four-drawer file cabinet
filled with my completed recent
files from the last six years."

Curtis was agreeable to that
set-up which meant that I wouldn't
have to store the old files in my
trailer.

On Tuesday the final deal of my
long career was duly completed
late in the morning and I did the
banking and disbursed the sale
proceeds.

For the rest of the week I
prepared and sent in the necessary
forms to formally retire from the

practice of law. I also closed out my business and trust bank accounts.

Curtis said that he'd let me know whenever any stray mail arrived at the office.

I weeded out files on the weekend to ensure that any old files which I left with Curtis were ones in which my purchaser clients still owned the property I had assisted them in buying. I also ripped up any sale files more than two years old.

By late Sunday afternoon I had reduced the files to just under a hundred and freed up one of the four drawers in that file cabinet.

I also packed into my car my computer and personal effects from the office and brought them to my trailer.

My legal career was now a relic of the past.

Tomorrow morning I'd hand in my office keys and collect the $500 from Curtis.

CHAPTER 3 (A Severe Downer)

On Monday morning I hit the office precisely at nine o'clock. This was the final day of my long career and it felt important to me not to arrive for work late.

Curtis was very gracious. He paid me the $500 plus the rent refund and said that he had decided to add my office space to his own. A carpenter was coming in tomorrow to create a doorway in one of the walls between our previously separate offices.

We spent an hour going over my closed-out files. Curtis seemed pleased with the weeding-out I had done over the weekend.

Finally at ten-thirty I handed him my office keys and bade him goodbye.

As I walked to my old clunker, I turned back and looked fondly at the building in which I had operated my business since the structure was erected in 1987. In fact I had practiced at the same address ever since becoming a lawyer in 1973. I had even articled for an older attorney in 1971 and 1972 at the former funeral home which had stood on this site before it was torn down to make way for the current building in 1987.

Instead of pride in having been an honest attorney for forty-seven full years, I was hit with an enormous sense of failure.

Despite having practiced in a lucrative profession for almost five decades, I was wallowing in poverty.

My automobile was a rusted-out 2002 Chevy Cavalier which I had owned ever since I bought it brand new in February of that year.

I drove east on Old Highway 2 for about five miles to the dumpy trailer park where I'd resided since 1999 when for $10,200 I bought the single-wide trailer from a bank which had seized it from the previous owner when he defaulted on his loan.

Now that my legal career was over, my only income was my Canada Old Age Pensions which brought in about $19,000 each year.

I had no retirement plan.

The good news was that the elimination of my office overhead meant that my monthly expenses were now very modest. The land rent for my trailer was only $300 per month. I had no internet service here because I had used my office computer to access the internet. My cable TV cost about $90 each month and my home phone was another $45.

As the day wore on, my mood soured.

This trailer park was not handy to any shopping area. When my old car conked out, purchasing a used replacement vehicle would be problematic.

Another crisis would occur if I needed significant dental work. The total savings in my bank checking account only amounted to $1,250 and that included the money I'd just received from Curtis.

It would have been nice to celebrate at the local casino tonight but that facility was closed for the two-week shutdown.

I cooked three frozen burritos for supper and then began my solitary retirement party by cracking open a beer.

By the third beer I had become quite morose.

For a while I'd watched TV but got sick of the hype over the coronavirus. The health lunatics had taken over the country and no one seemed concerned about the damage to the Canadian economy.

America was no better but at least that shutdown was more understandable. The Democrats could use the decimation of their country's economy to damage President Trump and prevent him from being re-elected in November.

Stock markets had taken a brutal shit-kicking over the past six weeks. The Dow Jones average had closed today just above 19,000. In early February it had topped 29,000.

It struck me that my own value was at its absolute career bottom right now.

Without my law office, I had no outside source of income which meant that I'd be mired in poverty for the remainder of my sorry life.

Even worse, now I had nothing with which to fill my time.

Would tomorrow be the first day in my entire life in which I poured beer on my Kellogg's All-Bran cereal?

By the time I'd quaffed four "celebratory" bottles of beer, I was completely depressed and feeling sorry for myself.

Was I the biggest legal failure since lawyers first emerged from the swamp thousands of years ago?

CHAPTER 4 (Protesting Old Lawyer)

On Tuesday morning I began my new life of leisure with a bad hangover. That didn't bode well for my future.

Since most businesses were closed because of the government shutdown, I stayed in the trailer.

Getting the internet service hooked up proved to be a hassle. Even though the service provider switched me on, I wasn't able to locate a local business which would come to my trailer and get my computer working here. I was a klutz whenever technology was involved.

Finally on Thursday I found a guy who agreed to come over and hook my computer up to the internet.

It cost $75 cash but at least now I could keep abreast of the news without relying on television.

On Friday morning Ontario's Premier Ford announced that the shutdown was being extended to April 15th.

That incensed me. No political debate had taken place and the public hadn't even been consulted.

Dire predictions were being tossed out by medical experts that millions of people could die from the pandemic and they warned that social distancing and business closures could continue indefinitely.

I had brought from my office ample paper and miscellaneous supplies.

Businesses which sold craft and office items had been declared essential so I drove up to Michael's in the north end of town and purchased two dozen sheets of thin white cardboard and a plastic sign holder into which I could fit my signs.

Back in the trailer I began creating some protest signs.

By two o'clock I had made four separate signs.

I drove to South Front Street and parked my car on the street in a spot where free parking was permitted.

Then I walked to City Hall.

Even though it was closed to the public, I began my one-man protest outside the front entrance.

The message I had printed out and displayed in the sign holder today said "OUR GOVERNMENT CAN'T AFFORD TO PAY US NOT TO WORK."

This was the first time in my life that I'd taken to the streets to protest anything.

Over the years I had occasionally written a letter to the editor or penned an article for the Law Times but today I was marching back and forth in front of Belleville City Hall expressing my anger with the decision to close down Canada's economy.

It was very quiet downtown since virtually all of the businesses were closed down. A disturbingly large number of stores were already empty, the victims of the long trend by successful enterprises to relocate in shopping malls where parking was free and plentiful.

As a result virtually no pedestrians walked past. The few who did ignored me and I noticed several folks crossing the street before they got to my location. Maybe they assumed I was a nut-job or a panhandler.

After two hours I gave up and walked back to my car.

It was highly discouraging. Not a single person had stopped to find out more details about my public complaint. Many motorists had slowed down to read my sign but only a handful had tooted their horns or given me the thumbs-up in support.

Apparently the fear of coronavirus had driven most people to hole up inside their homes and apartments until the infection curve had been flattened.

Fortunately the beer stores were considered essential services. I purchased two large cases of

Molson Export Canadian beer on my way back to the trailer park.

CHAPTER 5 (Biggest Loser)

For supper I made grilled cheese sandwiches.

Over the years I had gotten friendly with a couple of the residents but soon realized that my neighbors were non-working deadbeats living off government welfare or disability payments.

They only feigned friendship in order to drink my beer and we had nothing in common other than being losers who resided in a run-down trailer park. Now I was out-of-work and relying on my government checks just like them.

For the past several years I had kept to myself around here.

My best friend had died five years ago. The decades of relatively heavy drinking had finally caused his body to shut down at the age of sixty-eight. Jim had also been a real estate attorney. We had attended law school together and opened up our legal practices on the same month back in 1973.

Running my business had been a real struggle ever since Linda died.

A massive recession battered Canada beginning in the summer of 1990 just a few months after Linda had passed away.

My income had plummeted almost immediately and never recovered. To keep my overhead down, I never hired a secretary. Typing was the most valuable skill I had learned in high school and it enabled me to operate without staff after Linda was taken from me.

To fill my time after her death and give me something to look forward to, I had begun taking inexpensive one-week holidays on my own to Las Vegas every three or four months.

Those trips were my only indulgence and they at least managed to keep me sane.

I had kept the cost of the vacations way down by choosing cheap flights and staying in older hotels in the downtown section of Vegas.

Linda and I had never worried about saving up money for our retirement and we tended to spend almost every cent that came in, mostly on frequent vacations. We never purchased a home because we took so much time off.

That meant that I had very little in the way of savings when Linda died. I moved into increasingly more modest apartments in the years following her death until I finally decided to purchase this trailer in 1999. It was all I could do to scrape up the purchase money. I had to max out my credit card in order to come up with part of the cash. The bank refused to loan me any money secured by the trailer.

That lack of financial planning was going to haunt me now. I had no emergency savings.

When the Great Recession hit Canada and the USA in 2008, the bargains in Las Vegas abruptly came to an end. The casinos had by

then all switched to players'
cards which kept track of slot
play. I never again qualified for
any free rooms or meals since I
was a minimum bet slot player.

My vacations to Vegas dwindled
to once a year and it had become
more and more stressful to
navigate through the many airport
security rules.

My last trip had been at
Christmas in 2016 as an escape
from the loneliness of spending
the holiday season all alone in my
trailer.

It was doubtful that I'd ever be
able to scrounge up the price of
another holiday.

As it turned out, Lady Luck
hadn't totally abandoned me. A
casino opened here in Belleville
in January of 2017 and it had
several of the Caveman Keno
machines that I loved.

Since the casino opened, it had
become my main source of
entertainment.

A casino was a fantastic place
for an old guy who was on his own.

Nobody even noticed whether a slot player was gambling alone. Even eating at a table for one in the casino buffet or the Windward Restaurant was considered perfectly normal.

My mind drifted back to my City Hall protest. It had accomplished nothing, much like my legal career.

By the time I hit the sack after socking back three bottles of beer, I felt like the biggest loser in the history of the legal profession.

Just before I fell asleep the sad thought struck me that I was perhaps the only retired attorney in the world living in a dumpy trailer park.

Welcome to retirement life, Mr. Loser.

CHAPTER 6 (More Protesting)

I remained in a deep funk over the next couple of weeks. Doug Ford, the premier of Ontario had extended the shutdown yet again, this time to the middle of April.

Then two days before that period was set to expire, the bastard continued the lockdown until May 4th.

I was livid.

By then I'd been shocked to learn that both the Canadian and Ontario governments expected their annual budget deficits to be ten times the already lofty levels forecast before the pandemic hit.

The USA wasn't much better. The federal government under Donald Trump now forecast an annual budget shortfall of an incomprehensible four trillion dollars.

European countries were also running obscene deficits because of the shutdown of their economies.

It was fiscal insanity.

Just as sinister was my suspicion that the health officials were exaggerating the coronavirus statistics.

There seemed to be some gigantic plot by an unseen hand to drive all western economies into bankruptcy. Money no longer mattered.

In late April I dragged myself back downtown with my protest signs.

One sign screamed "END THE SHUTDOWN" and on the reverse side was the message "STOP GOVERNMENT OVERSPENDING."

Since there were virtually no pedestrians in the City Hall entrance area, I began walking up one side of Front Street and back down the other side.

That strategy paid better dividends.

Many folks who knew me personally stopped to listen to my

point of view but very few appeared to agree with me.

To them I was just an irrelevant old fart with too much time on his hands.

A reporter from the community newspaper took my photo and interviewed me.

The following Thursday on May 7th the article appeared in the publication.

Unfortunately the reporter took the position that I was badly misinformed.

The main thrust of the piece stressed the seriousness of coronavirus and in fact most of the quotes were from local medical workers who unanimously claimed that I was putting lives at risk by walking around downtown without wearing a mask.

Even the photo that the reporter used made me look cranky and somewhat disheveled. It had been windy that day and my hair was badly misbehaving.

The public mockery of my protest convinced me to give up and I spent the remainder of May pretty much holed up in my hot dump of a trailer. It had no air conditioning and May had been unusually warm this year. The two electric fans I had were grossly insufficient to keep me cool.

Retirement was not the carefree permanent vacation I had long ago assumed it was.

Being idle was incredibly boring. There was still nothing to do. The casino remained closed as did restaurants except for drive-through service. Even take-out was severely restricted. In any event, dining out even with relatively cheap take-out food was beyond my budget.

CHAPTER 7 (Counter-Protest)

A loosely organized group called Black Lives Matter had suddenly risen to the forefront of the American news.

They were active participants in the violent riots in many American cities but politicians and big business seemed terrified to upset the supporters of Black Lives Matter. Corporations donated tens of millions of dollars to the group and the media treated them like the second coming of Jesus Christ.

The lawlessness sickened me. I saw the bunch as domestic terrorists.

On June 5th I read in the on-line edition of the local newspaper than a Black Lives Matter support rally was being held in downtown Belleville on Sunday evening.

I was incensed. The bullshit had even reached small town Ontario.

The media had jumped on the bandwagon that Canada and America were somehow inherently racist. That was blatantly false and I decided to hold my own counter-protest.

I made up two new signs. One of them said "ALL LIVES MATTER" and the other stated "CANADA IS NOT RACIST."

I was about to leave for downtown when my anger overtook me and I created two additional signs with extra punch.

One of them said "WHITE LIVES MATTER TOO" and the other said "DON'T LISTEN TO THESE TERRORISTS."

In order to get the jump on the other protesters, I took my signs downtown on Saturday afternoon and paraded up and down Front Street with the first two less offensive signs, one facing from the front of the holder and the other from the rear.

The reactions I received were mixed. Older people often voiced their support of my signs but the younger generation seemed to revile me as some sort of red-neck bigot.

None of the kids who flung obscenities my way stopped to discuss the issues. They may as well have cut their own ears off. Presumably the schools had completely indoctrinated the kids to believe that liberal garbage.

On Sunday I took all four signs back downtown at three o'clock. The two more controversial signs were slotted in between the other two signs so were hidden from view. It was quite hot so I stood in a bit of shade in front of City Hall until the worst of the afternoon heat had subsided a bit.

The last thing I needed was to collapse from heat stroke in a pathetic puddle of failed protest.

More people were arriving to join the march which would begin about three blocks to the north of where I was standing. A few folks opted instead to stand and observe the march from the sidewalks on Front Street.

A group of seven teenagers spotted me shortly after quarter to six.

They surrounded me and tried to intimidate me with taunts.

"You're a disgusting bigot," one of them snarled.

"And you're full of shit, kid. You should learn to question the crap your teachers are feeding you. Canada is not a racist country and everyone should be treated equally, even morons like you."

That wasn't the response the kid was expecting and she let me have it with a string of obscenities and insults. I was impressed with her vocabulary.

"Is that the garbage they're teaching you spoiled brats these days? Go join the parade and get out of my face. You children deserve the pathetic and bankrupt government you're going to be stuck with."

That reply elicited another round of swear words.

"I hope your useless protest march doesn't run late. If it does then you're going to miss your seven o'clock Idiots Anonymous meeting."

The gang gave me the collective finger and departed in order to join the parade before it got underway.

Their attitude incensed me and I switched the soft message signs for the more in-your-face ones.

After a few minutes I began walking north in order to meet the protest march head-on.

CHAPTER 8 (Confrontation)

I made it just past Victoria Avenue when I heard the shouts emanating from the approaching parade.

By the time I made it to the Empire Theatre, the parade had rounded a bend and came into view.

I stopped and stood with my sign aloft while the marchers passed me.

My presence acted as a catalyst which turned the event from a festive parade into an angry confrontation.

Some of the leaders were incensed that I had the gall to rain on their parade with my "racist" signs.

They yelled insults and I hollered right back at them, calling them terrorists and reverse bigots.

The same group of seven teenagers were particularly

enraged at my presence and were my most vocal critics.

It hadn't been my intention to turn myself into a radical but the message these bozos were spewing turned my stomach.

Deciding that I'd made my point, I didn't follow the parade south on Front Street once it had passed me. It really wasn't a great turnout. There might have been a couple of hundred people marching and most of those appeared to be high school or university students. A few folks had dragged their younger kids along, presumably to teach them some perverted interpretation of "diversity."

Really there were very few onlookers. A handful of people were peppered here and there on the sidewalks but most folks who decided to come out had marched in the parade rather than view the event from the sidelines.

It struck me that despite having lived and worked in Belleville all my life, I didn't see a single person I recognized.

This could just as easily have been a protest in Dearborn, Michigan. I guess none of my clients or colleagues had drunk the systemic racism Kool-Ade.

I began to walk back to my vehicle which was parked on South Front Street just past the beer store.

When I was in sight of City Hall, I noticed that the crowd had gathered at the front entrance to hear speeches.

Coward that I was, I decided not to attempt to push my way past the audience. I walked a block east to Pinnacle Street and then headed south.

Unfortunately I'd been spotted.

The same group of teenagers I had encountered before pried themselves away from the speakers and apprehended me just as I passed the empty and derelict building that used to be the home of the local newspaper.

They herded me into the parking lot of the old building and began taunting me with various obscene slurs on my character.

Despite my better judgement, I retorted with my own insults demeaning their level of intelligence.

As anyone with an ounce of common sense could have predicted, it was folly to antagonize a mob, even a small group of spoiled college or high school brats.

They rushed me. One of the bigger idiots held me while the others vandalized my protest sign, ripping up the cardboard messages and breaking the plastic sign holder into as many pieces as they could manage.

CHAPTER 9 (Humiliation and Arrest)

The big lummox behind me who had me pinned with his powerful grip refused to release me.

That angered me and I lashed out verbally, the only weapon I had in my depleted arsenal.

"Don't the schools teach you morons to tolerate opposing points of view?" I shouted.

My query only further incited the mini-mob.

While the one boy maintained his firm hold to prevent me from moving, another kid approached me from the front.

"Tolerate this, you old racist," he screamed while he yanked my trousers and undershorts down to my ankles.

The crowd burst out in mocking laughter while every participant videoed my embarrassing genital exposure with their smart phones.

As if my luck couldn't possibly get any worse, two female police officers suddenly arrived to investigate the noisy incident.

A couple of the young women yelled out to the cops.

"This pervert is exposing himself. He should be arrested."

By the time the cops looked my way, the kid had released my arms and stepped back.

I was standing with my pants down and my privates on view for the world to see. I quickly pulled my underwear back up to shield the innocent from such a sad eyeful. An old man's genitals are just about the most pathetic thing imaginable and just as useless.

Then I tried to yank my trousers up. The kid who disrobed me had used such force that my pants dropped despite being held in place by a belt.

It was now necessary for me to undo the belt before I could get my trousers up over my hips.

The two cops sprang into action.

Before I knew what was even happening, one of the cops was

securing my wrists with handcuffs behind my back.

Meanwhile the crowd cheered.

"I'm the victim here," I protested. "One of these vile pukes held me while another guy pulled my pants down. The whole self-righteous group of onlookers videoed the entire episode on their phones. Don't let them leave until you've viewed their devices."

"We have no legal right to demand access to their phone records."

"Ask permission, you cretin. Don't they teach you anything at police school other than how to drive and eat doughnuts at the same time?"

The bystanders were getting a real kick out of my angry exchange.

They started chanting, "Jail the pervert" over and over again.

That attracted other interested spectators and before long the group witnessing me being arrested and stuffed in the back of a squad car was larger than the gaggle of gullible fools still listening to the systemic racism speeches.

I was driven the three or four blocks to the police station where I was formally charged and fingerprinted. No one even bothered to interview me which made me even angrier.

I demanded an immediate bail hearing and also insisted on speaking with a proper detective about the incident.

My requests were ignored and I was led to a small jail cell in the basement.

My frustration level rose to absurd levels and my entreaties that I was a retired attorney who was entitled to be heard fell on deaf ears. Most cops loathed lawyers.

No detective or anyone else arrived at my cell to hear my side of the story.

A submarine sandwich and container of apple juice was brought to me at six o'clock.

At ten o'clock I abandoned all hope and fell asleep on the small and uncomfortable cot.

CHAPTER 10 (It Gets Worse)

Surprisingly I slept soundly and didn't wake up until breakfast was delivered. The clock on the wall near my cell showed that it was eight o'clock.

The ridiculousness of my predicament was strangely amusing. At the ripe old age of seventy-two, Paul Lang had finally tasted prison time. I wondered if I had grown a pair of impressive biceps in the night.

Last evening the cops had read me my rights and advised that I could contact an attorney immediately. I declined their offer and snapped that I was perfectly capable of handling my own affairs.

The cop who fingerprinted me shot right back, "How's that working out for you so far?"

A woman dressed in civilian clothes arrived at my cell late in the morning.

"Good morning, Mr. Lang. My name is Detective Marcie Benton. I've just started my shift and was informed of your arrest last night. I understand that you're a local attorney."

"I retired in March."

"I've never heard of you. Did you just move to this area recently?"

"I've had my legal practice at 210 Church Street since I was called to the bar in 1973, but I never handled criminal matters. I restricted my practice to real estate transactions."

"I see. Unfortunately we've missed the opportunity to have your bail hearing today. The judge has already dealt with the case load from the weekend by video conference and has left her chambers for the remainder of the day. We've scheduled your hearing for tomorrow morning."

"I can live with that. My more pressing concern is for someone to investigate the incident. The officers who arrested me were stone deaf to my entreaties. I didn't expose myself. A big oaf from the mob grabbed me from behind and held me firmly. Then another kid yanked my trousers and underpants down to my ankles while the rest of the brats took pictures of my humiliating situation. I implored the arresting officers to interrogate the witnesses and view their smart phones, but they refused."

"I'm so sorry, Mr. Lang. I'll speak with the arresting officers today and see whether they managed to obtain the names of any of the witnesses."

I thanked the lady and she departed.

The rest of the day was boring. It seemed that I was the only prisoner in this section of the jail. My only subsequent visitors were employees delivering my meals.

Detective Benton returned early in the evening after I'd eaten supper.

"I don't have any good news, Mr. Lang. The arresting officers told me that they were so anxious to remove you from a potentially dangerous situation that they didn't speak with any of the witnesses or record any of their names. Even more damaging to your explanation, they actually saw you standing in front of the crowd with your genitals fully exposed."

"That is so bloody incompetent. I told the two morons what had happened but they totally ignored me."

"What started the confrontation?"

"I'd been hoisting my own counter-protest signs during the Black Lives Matter march. The small crowd accosted me while the speeches at City Hall were being given and forced me into the parking lot of the vacant newspaper building. We exchanged insults for a couple of minutes and then they grabbed me. I've already told you what happened from that point on."

"You're in a very precarious
situation, Mr. Lang. It would be
prudent for you to hire a criminal
attorney immediately. The judge
might decide not to grant you bail
tomorrow since the alleged crime
is of a sexual nature.
Theoretically you could even be
found guilty and deemed to be a
dangerous sexual offender."

"That's ludicrous. I'll take my
chances and defend myself. In fact
I might even launch an action
against your department. The two
cops who arrested me were grossly
negligent. I'm beginning to
question your own competence. I
expect that the entire episode is
already posted on YouTube. Haven't
you learned how to operate a
computer or did you miss that
class at police school because you
were on doughnut break?"

Benton burst out laughing.

"Generally folks on the inside
of a jail cell tend not to insult
the police detective who is
investigating the situation."

"Lawyers expect quality service. So far all I've seen from your department is infuriating negligence."

"I'll take a peek at the internet before I finish my shift."

Benton departed.

CHAPTER 11 (Public Shaming)

I didn't hear anything from Benton on Monday evening after our chat. Some drunks were brought in around midnight and that woke me up.

From time to time I was startled awake during the night to the sound of puking down the hall.

By morning I was exhausted because it hadn't been easy to get back to sleep after each rude interruption.

Additional incompetence greeted me on Tuesday.

The bail hearing judge had taken sick and no other judge could be found at the last minute to hear her cases.

It appeared that I'd be spending additional time in this depressing jail cell.

The time passed very slowly but at least there was a bit of entertainment today since there were other prisoners nearby and I eavesdropped on their conversations and arguments.

When my supper was delivered, there was a newspaper clipping from today's edition on my tray.

The article was abominable.

LAWYER'S RUDE COUNTER-PROTEST AGAINST BLACK LIVES MATTER MARCHERS

Local attorney Paul Lang decided to launch his own protest against the folks marching in support of BLACK LIVES MATTER on Sunday evening in downtown Belleville.

The elderly lawyer marched up and down Front Street in plain sight of the BLACK LIVES MATTER support parade. His own signs screamed "WHITE LIVES MATTER TOO" and "CANADA IS NOT RACIST."

As might be expected, a confrontation ensued.

That's when Lang decided to demonstrate the full range of his legal skills.

He pulled his pants down and exposed himself to the crowd.

*That rude gesture occurred at
the worst possible time for the
attorney. Two police officers
arrived at the precise moment when
Lang was displaying his privates
in their full glory.*

*Lang was arrested and is still
in jail awaiting a bail hearing.
Occasionally justice does prevail.*

*Doubtless Paul Lang will be
shocked at the legal fee levied by
his own defense attorneys. Lang
will soon find out why society
loathes lawyers so thoroughly.*

I couldn't believe it. The
damned reporter had penned the
story without even attempting to
speak with me.

My pristine reputation for
honesty, competence and probity
had taken me forty-seven years of
faithful legal practice to build.

Suddenly in a matter of forty-
eight hours I was unjustly branded
as a raving racist degenerate.

CHAPTER 12 (Good News, Bad News)

I was still in shock when
Detective Benton breezed into the
basement at eight o'clock on
Tuesday evening.

"I've finally got some good news
for you, Mr. Lang. We're dropping
all charges against you. Follow me
and the appropriate paperwork can
be processed."

I didn't even reply but tagged
meekly behind Benton.

"You don't seem excited about
regaining your freedom, Mr. Lang."

"Have you read today's
newspaper?"

"No I haven't. I don't subscribe
to it."

I handed the article to the
detective while we walked up the
stairs.

"I'm so sorry, sir. This is
absolutely terrible."

"I know. Believe it or not, I
was a totally honest attorney for
my entire career. Now the only

thing I'll ever be remembered for is being arrested for hanging a rat at a protest rally. It's very demoralizing."

"I took your advice and scoured YouTube. Just as you guessed, the entire confrontation is on the internet. Young people today can't resist the impulse to publicly post their various exploits. I made the two arresting officers watch the YouTube video and they asked me to convey their sincere apologies to you, Mr. Lang."

It took about thirty minutes to complete the administrative details and the police returned to me my wallet and keys.

I declined the offer of a ride to my automobile and walked the three blocks to where I had parked it.

That's when my life took another turn for the worse.

My car had been thoroughly vandalized. The tires had all been slashed, the windows broken and there was shit smeared all over the seats and dashboard.

Someone had left a sign saying "RACIST PIG" on the front seat.

I walked back to the police station and reported the crime. By then darkness had fallen.

The cop at the front desk let me use their phone to contact my insurance company to notify them of my claim. They advised me to have the vehicle towed to a wrecker's yard which I did but I had to walk back to the car to wait for the tow truck.

The tow cost $80. When I tried to use my credit card to pay the fee, the chap's machine wouldn't accept my card. The message kept coming up "REJECTED." I was forced to pay in cash.

That drained my wallet of enough cash to pay for a taxi. I had no choice but to walk the five or six miles back to my trailer.

As luck would have it, rain began falling by the time I reached Haig Road so I was drenched by the time I finally made it home.

No sooner had I unlocked the trailer door and stepped inside, when I noticed that water was pouring onto the kitchen floor from a leak in the roof above. I found a bucket and put it under the leak and then cleaned the accumulated water off the kitchen floor.

It seemed that the whole world was against me.

CHAPTER 13 (Despondent)

The motto of most lawyers can be summed up as "WHEN THE GOING GETS TOUGH, THE TOUGH GET DRUNK."

Attorneys are noted for having massive alcohol addiction problems.

I cracked open a beer and sat in the tiny living-room feeling sorry for myself.

Even though it was unwise given my sour mood, I pulled the folded-up newspaper article out of my wallet and reread it several times.

I used to have a pretty decent sense of humor, but that attribute had faded over the past several years. Twenty years ago I could have seen the humor in this situation and perhaps even have joked about it.

That ability had been beaten out of me by the many years of subsistence living at my law office.

Eventually even I came to realize that Paul Lang was a financial failure.

My legal practice income hadn't even topped $10,000 in any year since I turned sixty-five and began collecting my old age pensions.

In fact last year my office had only generated $3,000 in income after the overhead had been paid.

I went to my desk and dragged out my calculator. Most weeks last year I had put in about thirty-five hours per week at the office and hadn't taken any vacation.

That meant that my legal earnings were only $57.69 per week or a pathetic $1.65 an hour. I could have increased my wages ten-fold if I'd taken a job at Burger King.

This current year had been much worse and in fact I had lost several thousand dollars from January 1st to March 23rd when I retired. Winter is a terrible time for real estate lawyers and the few fees I generated were insufficient to pay my office overhead.

That realization only emphasized what a colossal failure I was.

Paul Lang had toiled in a lucrative profession for forty-seven years and had nothing to show for it except a newspaper article branding him as a racist pervert.

The insurance company had informed me that I was covered for the vandalism but that the vehicle wasn't worth repairing. They would pay me the blue book value of $500 and reimburse me for the towing charge.

Eighteen year old Chevrolet Cavaliers were effectively worthless.

Now I was stuck in a trailer park several miles from civilization without a vehicle.

The dilapidated trailer itself was also worth next to nothing and I had no money to repair or replace the roof.

At least I had lots of beer in the fridge and cupboards.

By the time I'd knocked back three bottles of beer, I arrived at the conclusion that life wasn't worth living.

I went into my bedroom closet and found my revolver and ammunition. I had purchased the gun several years ago for personal protection when a raft of violent home invasions had occurred in the Belleville area.

I loaded the gun and brought it into the kitchen where I sat at the small table in order to listen to the rainwater plopping into the bucket on the floor.

It was a pathetic situation.

After I'd polished off a bit more beer, I'd put myself out of my misery.

CHAPTER 14 (Surprise Visitor)

I must have read the newspaper piece another dozen times. Each perusal of the article acted like another nail in my coffin of confidence.

My reputation was irredeemable.

I'd be the laughing-stock of the legal profession and my former clients would be shocked to realize that they had sat across the desk from a pervert.

My reputation was really all I had to hang my hat on. I'd failed financially and I'd never done anything worthwhile in my whole career. I never had any important cases to win or even fight.

It was uncanny how one man could pretend to be a lawyer for forty-seven years and come up so empty.

I debated whether to open a fifth beer but couldn't even be bothered.

The time had arrived to put an end to my farce of a life.

I picked up the revolver and put the gun in my mouth.

Writing out some sort of suicide note would be futile. Nobody would give a shit why I blew my brains out. Besides, it would be disingenuous to blame the newspaper article and false arrest for my demise. I had no last will and testament. Like so many professionals, I had neglected my own legal affairs and never changed my will after Linda died.

Really it didn't matter because I had no close relatives left alive and had never been prone to give any money to charities which I believed to be a huge industry designed mainly to suck money out of the public. Besides, I had no estate to leave anyone anyway. Paul Lang was as close to penniless as an old man could get, relying solely on his government old age pensions.

It was the sum total of my useless life as Canada's biggest legal failure which was the trigger for my suicide. The arrest and humiliation were just bit players in the overall tragedy of the lonely and wasted thirty years since Linda was taken from me.

Just as I began to squeeze the trigger, suddenly a well-dressed young gentleman materialized standing in the kitchen facing me. He was wearing an expensive black pin-stripe suit and a very trendy tie. His hair was professionally styled and as he extended his hand to shake mine, I noticed a Gucci watch on his wrist.

For a moment I wondered if I had dozed off before firing the gun but realized that the gun was gripped firmly between my lips.

I removed the firearm from my mouth so that I could speak.

"This is a private party. You have no business crashing it," I barked.

"On the contrary, I've been sent here to persuade you not to give up on life."

"Who are you and who sent you?"

"My name is Desmond and I've been assigned to intervene in your situation."

"I don't require an intervention. Get out of my trailer."

"Surely as a veteran attorney, you've learned to obtain the facts before assessing your problem."

"The only fact that matters is that my reputation has been blown to shit and I'm old, poor and useless. Are you authorized to pay me a million dollars?"

"I'm afraid not. My role is merely to point out to you the benefits that you bestowed on your fellow humans during your lifetime."

"That won't take long. How do you plan to accomplish your task?"

"I'm in possession of a device which will allow you to view events that transpired as a direct result of your acts of wise counsel or human kindness."

"Are you supposed to be some kind of guardian angel?"

"That's one of the more common expressions used to describe me. It will suffice for the purpose of this meeting."

"I'll give you five minutes. After that I want you to bugger off."

CHAPTER 15 (Angelic Background)

"Five minutes will be more than enough time. What do you notice about the clock on your wall?"

"It cost a hell of a lot less than that watch on your wrist."

"That's a valid point."

"It raises another salient matter. Why did you drop in to my dumpy trailer dressed like a thousand bucks an hour legal shyster?"

"You're quite caustic. I've never encountered that attitude before. But then I've never been assigned to an attorney. My area of expertise has been more attuned to business leaders in the corporate boardrooms."

"What's your track record in saving those big-time crooks?"

"My success has been mixed, perhaps even more skewed to negative than to positive outcomes. But then those who attain that level of perceived success have more often than not hurt many folks along the path to the top of the food chain. I incorrectly assumed that as an attorney you would be more susceptible to the appearance of success."

"Every time you open your mouth, my distaste of you and your presence in my kitchen grows. I'm grabbing another beer and then you can start the show."

As I went to the fridge, I took out two bottles and removed both caps. When I handed a beer to my uninvited guest, he politely declined. That was another strike against the supercilious creep.

Someone who wouldn't even stoop to share a beer with a client who was about to kill himself didn't belong in my kitchen. I put the opened second beer back in my refrigerator to keep it cold. My innate frugality would now force me to drink that beer before sticking the revolver back in my mouth.

Desmond spoke.

"Please look at your wall clock again. What strikes you as odd about it?"

I examined the clock. At first I saw nothing unusual until it dawned on me that the second hand wasn't moving.

I clapped my hands in mock glee.

"I'm so impressed. You've stopped time just for little old me."

My guest wasn't amused and a scowl momentarily filled his face. He quickly recovered and shot me a dazzling smile.

"Where would you like to begin?" he asked.

"You can start by telling me about your angelic background. Were you ever a live person on this planet?"

"I'm afraid not. I belong to a completely different species."

"Feel free to drop the corporate titan look and reveal your true appearance."

"That isn't possible. My species has no corporeal existence. In terms you might comprehend, I'm composed solely of a complex combination of energy and cognition."

"How long have you been an angel?"

"In terms of your concept of time, I've been accepting assignments for the past four years."

"What were you doing prior to that?"

"I was studying and learning about humans since I came into being but I'm unable to tell you how long that process took. Time isn't a tangible concept in my reality. The education phase I've completed goes right back to my first awareness that I was alive."

"Tell me about some of your successful interventions."

"To do so is forbidden. We believe in the complete right of privacy."

"And yet here you are invading my privacy just when I was about to eat my gun. It seems that some folks' right to privacy is stricter than others."

"Clearly the Guiding Hand believes that your death tonight should be averted if possible. That's enough about me. Since you insist on being stubbornly uncooperative, I'll commence my presentation using the time-line of my own choosing."

CHAPTER 16 (Mr. Litigator)

"At least sit your ass down.
You're making me nervous standing
there like some talking statue."

The angel looked with disdain at
the other kitchen chair.
Apparently I hadn't noticed that
some of the leaked rain water had
splashed onto the seat.

"Your chair is filthy. I prefer
to stand."

"Is that expensive suit a
rental?"

"I don't understand your
question."

"Why would you give a shit
whether the suit gets dirty or
not? Once you're done here, you'll
presumably transform back to your
own species and the clothes you're
wearing will disappear like my
beer just did."

I stood up and fetched the beer
I had opened earlier for Desmond.
I was definitely feeling the
effects of so much beer.

Since the angel had no intention of sitting down for his presentation, I barked at him to get started.

Desmond began the show back when I was an inexperienced young attorney.

It was far more than a slide show. Desmond was able to take me right back to any moment in my life.

I watched myself sitting at my office desk. My father had purchased the old desk for $10 from Northern Electric, the company he worked for during his entire career. Dad had glued a thin sheet of hard decorative backing to the top of the desk and to the tops of a couple of old tables. The backing was in the design of white marble and was fully washable. Dad had done a great job because the fake marble tops had never become unglued during my entire forty-seven year legal career.

I had painted the wooden portion of all three pieces black and wound up using that desk and the two tables in my law office for my entire career. Curtis was now the "proud" owner of the furniture since I had no room for any of it in this dinky house trailer.

The young couple sitting in two inexpensive office chairs across from me were my new clients who had been shafted two years earlier by their realtor, a top-selling weasel named Bobby Crofton. He had persuaded them to purchase one of his own properties in the country even though it had no water supply. A scuzzy local lawyer had represented both Crofton and the purchasers. Crofton had taken back a mortgage since no bank would lend money to a home without a well. Water had to be trucked in.

The mortgage had come due two years later and the young couple had been unsuccessful in finding a bank or finance company which would lend them the funds to pay off Crofton's mortgage and the weasel refused to extend the term of the loan.

Crofton had commenced a lawsuit against the young couple and I agreed to handle their case.

I tried mightily to right the wrong but came up short. The judge rejected my argument that the young couple had been the victims of an egregious conflict of interest and he found in favor of Crofton. He also made no award as to costs which meant that each side had to pay their own legal account.

After the unfavorable judgement was rendered, Crofton's attorney and I came to an agreement whereby my clients would sign the home over to Crofton and forfeit any equity they had in the property.

I felt so bad about my failure that I'd only charged the clients for the disbursements I had expended and waived my legal fee even though I had spent many hours on the file.

That was also my last attempt at being Mr. Litigator. My courtroom skills were so lacking that I couldn't even emerge victorious in a case where the equities were so heavily in my clients' favor.

"Is watching this rerun of my courtroom failures supposed to make me change my mind about blowing my brains out?" I snapped.

"Of course not, but this device enables us to see what would have happened to your clients if you had refused to represent them. Are you interested in seeing that?"

"I guess so. I did turn them down at first but they were so upset at what was happening to them that I reluctantly changed my mind."

"Then let's watch the fate of the young couple in the scenario where you refused to represent them."

"Is this an alternate reality?"

"No it's not. Your reality is the only true version of events, but my device enables us to see how the true reality would have been altered if you had acted differently."

This time I was not persuaded to change my mind. The young couple left my office and wound up using another local attorney I never liked or trusted.

He pumped them full of false hope, drained their savings to pay his retainer, took a second mortgage on their home early in the litigation process and thoroughly milked the poor kids. The judge's ruling was remarkably similar but the clients had to declare bankruptcy because their attorney wouldn't agree to discharge his second mortgage without substantial payment. As a result, Bobby Crofton had to sell the home under power of sale rather than take back the title and that left a substantial shortfall.

The young couple divorced shortly after the bankruptcy and the woman became an alcoholic.

Desmond shut off the device and we were back in my kitchen.

"In real life, your clients stayed together, had children and continue to live a happy and productive life. As you can clearly see, what you perceived as a crushing courtroom failure was in fact a stunning victory."

"I'm impressed. I knew the kids had stayed together because I represented them over the years on several real estate transactions."

CHAPTER 17 (Panhandlers
Everywhere)

"Just how upset are you that you
never attained financial success?
Is that why you're contemplating
suicide tonight?"

It was a valid question and I
pondered it for a moment before
responding.

"I've always been a frugal kind
of guy so the absence of wealth
really didn't make much difference
to me. I guess it was the
comparison between my financial
circumstances and that of every
other attorney on the planet that
made me feel like a total failure.
That overall end result hurt my
pride. Coming last out of 20,000
lawyers in the Province of Ontario
alone isn't cause to celebrate, at
least for members of my generation
which believes that winning
matters."

"When I was studying your
circumstances prior to being sent

on this assignment, I was quite impressed with your generosity," Desmond mentioned.

"Are you out of your mind? I've never been generous with anyone. I don't donate to any charities and have never helped out at a food bank or done any community volunteer work. I think you've been studying the file of a different Paul Lang."

"You were certainly both kind and generous in this instance."

Desmond then whisked me into another episode from my past.

It was a hot Saturday morning in the summer and I was in my office working on some files.

As I was walking out to my car shortly before noon to grab some lunch, I happened to notice a man walking toward me from the church next door. He had parked in the office lot since the Bridge Street United Church had no parking lot of its own.

The man went to his car but seemed agitated. I watched myself with great curiosity. This incident had taken place around 1999.

"Are you looking for something?" I asked politely. "Perhaps I can help you."

"My family and I are heading out west from New Brunswick but we ran out of money and need to buy gas. I was hoping that the church would be open and could assist us. I already tried the Salvation Army but they were closed."

I watched my younger self open my wallet and give the man every cent I had on me which was $40.

He thanked me and mentioned that they had friends in Toronto who would be able to provide them with funds with which to make it out to Alberta. He then moaned that his family hadn't eaten anything today and that the car was unbearably hot because it didn't have air conditioning.

I whipped back into my office and brought out some potato chips and several cans of Vanilla Coke which had been in the tiny bar fridge in my office.

The man's young daughter ran up and hugged me before they drove off.

Desmond switched off the device and we were back in my kitchen.

"That family made it safely to Toronto and eventually out west. Trust me when I tell you that they would have met a tragic fate if you hadn't been so accommodating to their situation."

"That's good to know."

"I have several other examples of your generosity. It seems that during your trips to Las Vegas, you helped out a slew of panhandlers."

"Times were tough in the nineties," I replied. "It was hard to walk even a block or two without getting hit up for a handout. Are you going to tell me that some of those deadbeats turned their lives around because I tossed them five bucks?"

"Unfortunately nothing noteworthy ensued as a direct result of your largesse. Your actions do reflect nicely on your

character. Very few of my rich
assignments ever showed such
generosity of soul. I must admit
that I was touched by your
kindness to those complete
strangers."

CHAPTER 18 (Worthless Kindness)

"Desmond, I'd like you to show me any situations in which my involvement turned out to have negative consequences. Can you do that?"

"I suppose I could but I'm most reluctant to do so. No one has ever made such a request of me."

"Indulge me. I once gave an old woman fifty or sixty bucks when she laid a sob story on me. It happened years ago, perhaps around 2002 at my office and I always wondered if she was conning me. Show me that encounter."

"I'd rather not. It's best to focus on the positive outcomes."

"Sorry, but I like to hear both sides of an argument before rendering a judgement. Lay it on me."

This story began much like that of the family heading out west.

Again it was late on a hot Saturday summer morning and I was working at my office when the buzzer sounded.

I went into the main hallway and unlocked the front entrance door to the building.

A tiny old lady explained that she had tried to obtain help at the church next door but it was closed. She was on a train from out west heading for Nova Scotia. She had run out of money and was ravenously hungry so she hopped off the train when it stopped at Belleville and decided to find a church which would give her some food or some money to buy food. She intended to catch the next train at three o'clock and continue her journey home.

I gave her $50 and drove her back to the train station which was about twenty blocks away. Then I gave her another ten bucks which completely drained the cash in my wallet. She thanked me profusely and I continued on home, quite pleased with myself for helping an old lady in need.

"Are you sure you want to continue?" Desmond queried.

I nodded but was already thinking that I was going to be outed as a gullible sucker.

That's precisely what happened.

I watched in disgust as the old bat peeked out the door of the train station to make sure I was gone. Then she walked about three blocks to the liquor store where she met up with two deadbeats.

They retired to a shady spot on Great St. James Street at the bottom of a steep wooden staircase. The location was only a block from the liquor store and was a prime spot for local alkies to get hammered.

The three of them drank up my sixty bucks in less than an hour at which point Desmond and I followed the woman to a low-income apartment complex just up the street from the train station.

The woman proceeded to puke up whatever portion of the liquor she had overindulged with.

I grinned at the angel.

"No good deed goes unpunished, Desmond. Remember that when you're intervening in future lives."

"It's sad but true that some acts of kindness turn out to be worthless. Let's examine some more of your successes."

CHAPTER 19 (A Loving Husband)

Desmond reactivated his device and this time we were transported to Linda's hospital room in February of 1990.

Sadly I recalled the depressed funk I experienced this past February 3rd when I woke up and realized that Linda had been gone for a full thirty years.

"Unlike virtually all of my previous assignments, you had a very amenable marriage without so many of the common thorns which tend to prick the marital bubble of happiness."

"It was mostly Linda's doing. She was a perfect fit for me. With all the failures I experienced in other aspects of my life, I did manage to remain a faithful and loving husband. In fact I've never even dated anyone since Linda died."

"You appeared to live a very satisfying life during the years you were together. I noticed many holidays during my studies of your file."

"We opted to live for the moment. Linda and I never purchased a home but instead decided to rent an apartment so that we could spend our money on frequent holidays. Linda and I rarely took expensive trips although we did fly to Hawaii twice and managed three Caribbean cruises. Most of our vacations were one-week jaunts down to Las Vegas which turned out to be very low-cost because we stayed at downtown hotels and took advantage of specials. We were extremely disciplined gamblers and never lost much money. We both loved Vegas and getting away for a week every three months was effective in keeping the stress level at the office manageable. Linda was my legal secretary during the entire ten years and two months we were married."

"Were you crushed that you never had children?"

"Neither Linda nor I possessed any parental instincts. We would have liked to have pets but decided that we took too many holidays to be proper pet owners. It wouldn't have been fair to our cats or dogs to be stuck in a vet's cage every time we flew off somewhere."

"As I was studying your situation, I was certainly aware of the pain you experienced when Linda got sick and passed away. I also witnessed how devastated you were four months ago when the thirtieth anniversary of her death passed. Is that painful memory the real cause of your impulsive decision to take your own life tonight?"

"Linda has nothing to do with it. My current circumstances now that I've retired have managed to trigger my pending suicide."

"Whenever I take the form of a human, I'm also infused with human feelings and emotions. I must admit that your accommodation arrangements are pitiful. I don't know how you tolerate living like this."

"I'm a guy on his own and like many old men, I don't put much stock in knickknacks or fancy furniture. Don't take this the wrong way, but how do your bosses expect you to carry out an effective intervention when the only humans you've interacted with have been rich pricks?"

"Apparently it is exceedingly rare for a lawyer to be deemed worthy of an intervention. No one had any experience with attorneys. I was selected because it was believed that my assignments with corporate giants would be the most relevant."

"Far be it for me to give advice, but I'd hazard a guess that having empathy for the specific circumstances of your clients would be a prerequisite for success. You refuse even to sit down with me because doing so might soil your suit. That makes it seem that visiting me is an unwelcome chore rather than a blazing act of mercy."

"I'll definitely consider your advice. Thank you for sharing your thoughts with me. Is there any aspect of your marriage that you'd like to revisit before I depart?"

"Linda and I took a trip to Las Vegas during the Christmas week of 1989. We stayed at the El Cortez downtown and on Christmas Eve both of us hit decent jackpots on adjoining Caveman Keno slot machines. I'd like to relive a portion of that evening."

Desmond accommodated me and I was able to recreate the feeling of euphoria Linda and I felt when we each scored jackpots of $204 within ten minutes of each other. In addition to the hand-paid cash, we were also given a coupon for an El Cortez jacket. We proudly wore those jackets during the remainder of the trip.

Unbeknownst to us, it would be the final vacation we ever took together.

Three weeks after returning home, Linda was diagnosed with a brain tumor and died on the operating table on February 3rd, 1990.

Reliving the dual jackpots infused me with a rush of love for my darling.

I can't honestly say that I ever experienced a single truly happy day in the thirty years since Linda died.

CHAPTER 20 (Goodbye Cruel World)

I thanked the angel for allowing me to revisit the Las Vegas trip.

Desmond obviously felt that his work here was done.

"I trust that my presence here tonight has persuaded you that the best is yet to come. I wouldn't have been sent if my bosses hadn't determined that you still had something to offer humanity."

"You have given me much to think about, Desmond. I'll put my gun back in the closet now before you leave. Thank you for taking the time to intervene."

I returned the revolver to the bedroom closet shelf and returned to the kitchen.

Desmond seemed quite pleased with himself. I wondered if the self-satisfied smirk on his angelic face was because he believed that he had successfully convinced me not to kill myself, or whether instead it was because he'd completed his assignment without soiling his business suit.

"Before you leave, I'd like your assessment of my abilities as an attorney. You appear to know more about me than anyone, possibly even more than I can remember myself."

"How candid do you want me to be?"

"I'd prefer an honest opinion, not a sugar-coated pile of bullshit. In other words, don't hand me a turd you've painted pink and tell me that it's cotton candy."

"Are you certain that's what you want?"

"Yes."

"In my opinion as an observer of your life, my conclusion is that you were too afraid of taking risks yourself and that tainted your legal advice to your clients. You talked far too many of your clients out of entering into entrepreneurial arrangements."

"Can you give me an example?"

Desmond switched his device back on and I saw myself advising a client that purchasing a carpet-cleaning franchise would be extremely risky.

The chap followed my advice and remained at his current job.

Desmond's device revealed that if the man had rejected my advice, he would have become a very successful business owner.

"Was that the only example you could come up with?"

"I could reveal at least a dozen similar situations. On the other hand, your conservative advice did turn out to be correct in many other instances. I have a bias in favor of risk takers since my experience as an angel has been focused on captains of industry who tend to be the ultimate gamblers."

"I recently read that Richard Branson's empire was created in large part because of his philosophy of risk taking which could be summarized as 'SCREW IT. LET'S DO IT.' He also credits his many failures with providing him with the experiences to ultimately be successful. Are you saying that I should have thrown caution to the wind when advising my clients?"

"My opinion is irrelevant. What's done is done, Paul Lang. It's too late for you to change the past. I'm here tonight merely to influence your decision to take your own life."

"I appreciate the visit, Desmond. Thank you for coming."

Desmond disappeared into thin air and I was again left alone.

The roof was still dripping water into the bucket which was almost full.

I emptied it into the kitchen sink and placed the bucket back under the leak.

Despite the copious bottles of beer that I'd consumed, I felt like one last drink to cap off the evening.

As I sipped the beer, my thoughts analyzed the images which Desmond had shown me tonight.

The clock on the wall was functioning again and in fact it was only a few minutes past the time when I had stuck the pistol in my mouth.

I began to ruminate about the evening. I highly doubted if Paul Lang had anything worthwhile to accomplish in the future. That was just a catchy phrase that Desmond had tossed out to impress me.

A decade or two of poverty-filled monotony was my likely lot in life.

I'd never been a religious believer except perhaps when I was a young kid and accepted whatever crap adults fed me.

One thing was clear to me tonight. Desmond hadn't been sent by God. No God worthy of the title would send a pompous snob to save a reject like Paul Lang. This angel or whatever he actually was found me and my surroundings distasteful. Why he was even sent would remain a mystery. His heart, if his species even had one, wasn't in this assignment.

I reflected again on my future prospects.

Even getting to the casino would be a major hassle from now on. Without a car, I'd have to pay for a cab or walk the three or four miles to the nearest bus stop on Haig Road.

The rain had gotten heavier again and the repetitious drip, drip, drip was obscenely annoying.

Every drop sounded like the word "LOSER."

I stood up and retrieved the gun from the bedroom closet.

With the loaded gun on the table in front of me, I continued to sip my beer and lament about my sad, lonely life. Every time I ventured out in public, folks would want to avoid the disgusting and disgraced old pervert. That would turn any trip to the grocery store or to the casino into an embarrassing nightmare.

As I drained the last bit of beer into my throat, I made up my mind.

I had been right the first time before the angel barged in on my private party. Paul Lang had run his course on this planet and it was time to cash in my chips.

I picked up my gun, walked outside in the rain and plunked myself on the wet ground in my tiny fenced-in back yard.

At least by terminating myself out here, no one would have to clean up a mess in my kitchen.

That was so typical of Paul Lang. He was considerate of others to the very end.

Goodbye, cruel world. You finally managed to crush me.

I put the firearm into my mouth, pulled the trigger and blew my brains all over the weed-infested yard.

CHAPTER 21 (Angelic Lesson)

Desmond had returned to his own sphere of existence, relieved that the task had been successfully completed.

Surely his bosses would be pleased with his latest intervention.

The council of elders suddenly appeared to collect their device.

The leader spoke.

"Was the intervention successful?"

"Yes it was. Paul Lang put away his gun and lived to fight another day. I trust that you are pleased with my results this time around."

"Actually the council is satisfied. Would you like to observe what transpired after your departure from Paul Lang's living quarters?"

"Yes, by all means, please inform me."

The device was activated and Desmond watched in utter

consternation as Paul Lang retrieved the gun from the other room and shortly thereafter went out in the yard and completed his successful suicide.

"I'm shocked. I was so certain that my presentation had changed Paul Lang's mind. I'm so sorry to have failed you."

"Think nothing of it. Paul Lang was of absolutely no consequence to the progress of humanity. The council utilized his situation in order to enable you to learn some valuable lessons for use in the future when the subject of our intervention really matters."

"I don't understand."

"As you study the entire episode, and with the advice we provide to you now that our own analysis has been completed, we fully expect you to be much more effective in future interventions."

"I appreciate your confidence in me, esteemed members of council."

The device replayed the events beginning with Desmond's

appearance in the kitchen of the house trailer.

After the shot was fired and Paul Lang lay dead and disfigured on the wet ground, the leader proceeded with the lesson.

"There are two related areas in which you need to improve your presentation. Paul Lang apprised you of one shortfall. As he so caustically pointed out, you lacked empathy both in your appearance and your conduct. Have you spotted those defects?"

"I've only noticed one of them, leader. I should have worn attire more in keeping with the poverty of the subject and I should have accepted his offer of a beverage and sat down at the table with him."

"That is correct. The other lesson is far more subtle. Merely sharing a beer and dressing in clothing appropriate to fit in to the intervention setting would improve your presentation on a superficial level and I'm sure you'll comply with those matters in the future."

"I'll certainly strive to do so, leader and members of council. Please instruct me as relates to the more complex lesson arising out of the ashes of my failure."

"You need to learn how to fake the appearance of having genuine concern for the fate of your subjects. Many successful politicians on Paul Lang's planet have mastered the art of lying with perfect delivery. The intonation of your words, the genuine look of complete empathy and the timing of the delivery must all coincide in order to have optimum effect on the subject."

"I'll undertake an intensive study of some of the political giants, leader. My goal will be to make Paul Lang my final failure and to learn from my mistakes on his file."

"That is why we sent you there in the first place. None of us cared what happened to that pathetic old drunk. But we were

concerned that a future inventor
or someone else who matters might
fail to be persuaded by your
intervention presentation."

"I'll do my utmost never to let
you down again. Thank you for
providing me with this opportunity
to improve."

CHAPTER 22 (Back at the Trailer Park)

Although the suicide shot was heard by several residents of the trailer park, no one called the police. A couple of folks poked their heads outside for a moment but concluded that the noise must have been a clap of thunder.

In fact it was several days before Paul Lang's body was discovered in his weed-infested rear yard.

No one was interested in administering his estate and no last will and testament was located.

The Public Trustee of Ontario was the entity deemed appropriate to look after Lang's estate.

They soon discovered that the trailer was too fragile to move so an agreement was reached with the owner of the park. He took title to the beat-up trailer and all its possessions in exchange for $2,000.

By September 1st the ownership had been transferred and the park owner rented out the trailer to a welfare deadbeat who was a friend of another resident.

Carl Stankowski, the park owner, lamented to his wife that now every unit in the trailer park was occupied by someone on government welfare or disability.

"Who else would live in that filthy cesspool, Carl? You now own every single trailer in the place but you haven't spent a cent on up-grades. Nobody is going to live there unless it's their very last option before knocking on the door of the homeless shelter."

There was no funeral for Paul Lang and no obituary was placed in the local newspaper.

The Public Trustee did run a notice for three successive weeks in July requiring any creditors of Lang's estate to file their notice of claim before August 1st.

Curtis Black, the lawyer who had purchased Paul Lang's office equipment, wasn't even aware of Paul's death until he read the Notice to Creditors in the local community newspaper. By then Lang had long since been cremated at the instructions of the Public Trustee.

Curtis had read the article about Paul's arrest for exposing himself in public but opted not to phone his long-time former tenant about the matter. He felt that Paul would be too embarrassed to want to talk about it.

Life went on for the residents of Belleville.

A few former clients and legal colleagues had given Paul Lang a bit of sad thought when they read the newspaper article about his lewd behavior. For those who spotted the Notice to Creditors and realized that the old lawyer had died, they likely believed that it was for the best. Nobody thinks highly of a pervert.

It was not an understatement to say that the elderly lawyer would not be missed by anyone in Belleville or elsewhere.

The leader of the council of angels had been correct.

In death and in life, veteran attorney Paul Lang had been of no consequence.

THE END

ABOUT THE AUTHOR

Donald W. Desaulniers is a retired Canadian lawyer who operated his own legal practice in the small city of Belleville, Ontario from 1973 until 2009. He is a graduate of University of Waterloo (1968) and University of Western Ontario Law School (1971). Donald still resides in Belleville with his lovely British wife, Jane and their cat Charlie.

Always a proponent of quantity over quality, Donald has published more than 75 novels, each of which is available exclusively on Amazon.

Listed below are all those "literary treasures" for your reading pleasure. The author hopes you enjoy his quirky sense of humor.

Happy reading everyone!

OTHER BOOKS BY THIS AUTHOR

SLIMY LAWYER SERIES

SLIMY LAWYER (#1 in Series)
SLIMY SUES AMERICA (#2 in Series)
SLIMY GETS SHAFTED (#3 in Series)
SLIMY GETS DISBARRED (#4 in Series)
SLIMY TASTES THE GOOD LIFE (#5 in Series)
SLIMY LAWYER CHECKS OUT (#6 in Series)

VANISHING LAWYER SERIES

VANISHING LAWYER #1 (A World Without Me)
VANISHING LAWYER #2 (Unwanted Witness)
VANISHING LAWYER #3 (Fugitive Alien)
VANISHING LAWYER #4 (Saving the President)
VANISHING LAWYER #5 (Swindling Seniors)
VANISHING LAWYER #6 (Saving Trump Again)

WEIRD LAWYER SERIES

WEIRD LAWYER #1 (Novice Attorney)
WEIRD LAWYER #2 (Tough Times)
WEIRD LAWYER #3 (A Pinch of Jealousy)

SNARKY LAWYER SERIES

THE WRONG LAWYER (#1 in Series)
SNARKY LAWYERS (#2 in Series)

LAWYER MURDER MYSTERIES

PARADE OF DEAD LAWYERS
SHUT THAT LAWYER UP
DIE NOW OLD MAN
LUCKY LAWYER
THE TWIN SHADOWS
TERRORIST LAWYER

LAWYER LOVE STORIES

BEVY OF BEAUTIES (Finding Love After Loss)
LOATHING THE LAWYER, LOVING THE LAWYER
NAÏVE LAWYER
REVENGE DELAYED
THE LORD SNATCHES AWAY
DIVERGENT LAWYER
THE CHEAPSKATE TWINS
BROKE, DISGRACED AND ALONE
LOVE SEDUCES A FOOL
A RETIRED LAWYER'S DOOMED ROMANCE

OTHER LAWYER NOVELS

LADY LUCK LOVES LAWYERS
RICH LAWYER, POOR PRIEST
TEMPTING THE GOOD LAWYER
LAWYER IN THE TOILET
FAKE LAWYER
BUYING REDEMPTION
THE CHRISTMAS LAWYER
THE LAWYER'S MUSLIM NEIGHBORS

OTHER ROMANCE NOVELS

SWEET ROMANCE BACK HOME
LOVE SAVES A LONER

SCIENCE FICTION

ALIEN SPECTATORS

TY WARD ADVENTURE SERIES

TY WARD HITS AMERICA (#1 in Series)
TY WARD'S HOLIDAY FROM HELL (#2 in Series)
TY WARD'S NEXT WAR (#3 in Series)
DEADLY WITNESS (#4 in Series)
A YOUNG HOOKER'S THANKS (#5 in Series)
TY WARD'S LAST WAR (#6 in Series)

TY WARD'S SHATTERED PEACE (#7 in Series)
TY WARD'S ROUGH JUSTICE (#8 in Series)

OTHER ACTION NOVELS

WARD JONES #1 (Fledgling Predator)
ESCAPE FROM EVERYTHING
CROSSING A RICH MAN (Turning the Tables)
VILE FAMILIES
MARTY MARCOTTE'S REVOLVING LIFE
THE LEFT TACKLE'S CHRISTMAS
FIFTY YEARS LATER (Hitchhiking in Donald
Trump's America)

SCHOOLBOY/BAWDY HUMOR

LOVE MOCKS A LIMP DICK (War of the Sexes)
CRAZY OLD LAWYER (A Talking Skin Tag)

YOUNG ADULT NOVELS

MYSTERY OF THE OLD DESK
CELESTIAL COINCIDENCE
YOUNG BUT NOT STUPID

NON-FICTION ESSAY

ADVICE TO STUDENTS FROM AN OLD FART (Surviving
University)

NOVELS WRITTEN UNDER PEN NAME "DURWARD GARBAGE"

WRONG PLACE, WORST TIME
ABANDONED ALIEN (Space Aliens for Donald
Trump)
GOLDEN CHAOS (Stock Market Meltdown)
NASTY MAN (Mr. Jerk)
ALMOST A LAWYER

SQUANDERING MY FORTUNE
REVENGE FROM HER GRAVE
LAWYER ON THE RUN (Panhandling Attorney)
SCORNFUL FAMILY (Eating Insults)

www.ingramcontent.com/pod-product-compliance
Lightning Source LLC
Chambersburg PA
CBHW030551130626
46552CB00006B/2504